Elephants & Emus

and Other Animal Rhymes

Conceived, designed, and produced by
Barefoot Books Ltd.
PO Box 95, Kingswood, Bristol BS15 5BH UK

First published 1997 in the United States of America by
Charlesbridge Publishing
85 Main Street, Watertown, MA 02172-4411
(617) 926-0329

Printed in Hong Kong
10 9 8 7 6 5 4 3 2 1

Library of Congress Cataloging-in-Publication Data is available upon request.

The illustrations in this book are done in watercolor.
The display type and text type were set in Gill Sans and Futura by Design/Section.
Color separations were made by Grafiscan, Italy.
Printed and bound by South Sea International Press Ltd.

Elephants & Emus
and Other Animal Rhymes

Collected and illustrated by

Philippa-Alys Browne

Charlesbridge

An elephant goes like this and that,
He's terribly big and he's terribly fat.
He has no fingers, he has no toes,
But goodness gracious, what a nose!

—Anonymous

The long-haired yak has long black hair,
He lets it grow—he doesn't care.
He lets it grow and grow and grow,
He lets it trail upon the stair.

—*William Jay Smith*

Down in the grass, coiled up
in a heap,
Lies a fat snake, fast asleep.
When he hears the grasses blow,
He moves his body to and fro.
Up and down and in and out,
Watch him slowly move about!
Now his jaws are open, so—
Ouch! He's caught my finger!
Oh!

—*Anonymous*

I think mice
Are rather nice.
Their tails are long,
Their faces small,
They haven't any
Chins at all.
Their ears are pink,
Their teeth are
    white,
They run about the
    house at night.
They nibble things
They shouldn't
    touch
And no one seems
To like them much.
But I think mice
Are nice.

—Rose Fyleman

The Big Baboon is found upon
The plains of Cariboo:
He goes about with nothing on
(A shocking thing to do).
But if he dressed respectably
And let his whiskers grow,
How like this Big Baboon would be
To Mr. So-and-So!

—Hilaire Belloc

Mud, mud, glorious mud,
Nothing quite like it for cooling the blood!
So follow me, follow
Down to the hollow
And there let us wallow
In glorious mud!

—*Anonymous*

A marvelous bird is the pelican,
Whose beak can hold more than his belly can.

—Ogden Nash

The true chameleon is small—
A lizard sort of thing;
He hasn't any ears at all
And not a single wing.
If there is nothing on the tree
'Tis the chameleon you see.

—*Carolyn Wells*

The Rhino is a homely beast,
For human eyes he's not a feast,
But you and I will never know
Why Nature chose to make him so.
Farewell, farewell, you old rhinoceros,
I'll stare at something less prepoceros.

—Ogden Nash

The lion, the lion, he dwells in the waste,
He has a big head and a very small waist;
But his shoulders are stark, and his jaws
        they are grim,
And a good little child will not play
        with him.

—*Hilaire Belloc*

Have you ever seen a Snail
Going off for walks,
With his house upon his back
And his eyes on stalks?
Well, when he has finished,
He rolls them in his head,
And goes inside his tidy house
And tucks himself in bed.

—Rodney Bennet

If I were a bear
And a big bear too,
I shouldn't much care
If it froze or snew;
I shouldn't much mind
If it snowed or friz—
I'd be all fur-lined
With a coat like his!

—A. A. Milne

If you should meet a crocodile,
Don't take a stick and poke him;
Ignore the welcome in his smile,
Be careful not to stroke him.
For as he sleeps upon the Nile,
He thinner gets and thinner;
Whene'er you meet a crocodile
He's ready for his dinner.

—Anonymous

The emu is a funny bird,
The way she runs is quite absurd;
Her legs are long, her body's round,
And however she tries, she can't leave the ground.

—*Stella Blackstone*